Louise C. Whitelock

Indian Summer

autumn poems and sketches

Louise C. Whitelock

Indian Summer
autumn poems and sketches

ISBN/EAN: 9783337370794

Printed in Europe, USA, Canada, Australia, Japan

Cover: Foto ©Andreas Hilbeck / pixelio.de

More available books at **www.hansebooks.com**

Indian Summer

Autumn

Poems and Sketches

L. Clarkson.

To American poets only
I am indebted for
these verses, and to
the woods of Maryland
for the studies.

New York
E. P. Dutton & Company
39 West 23rd St.
1883.

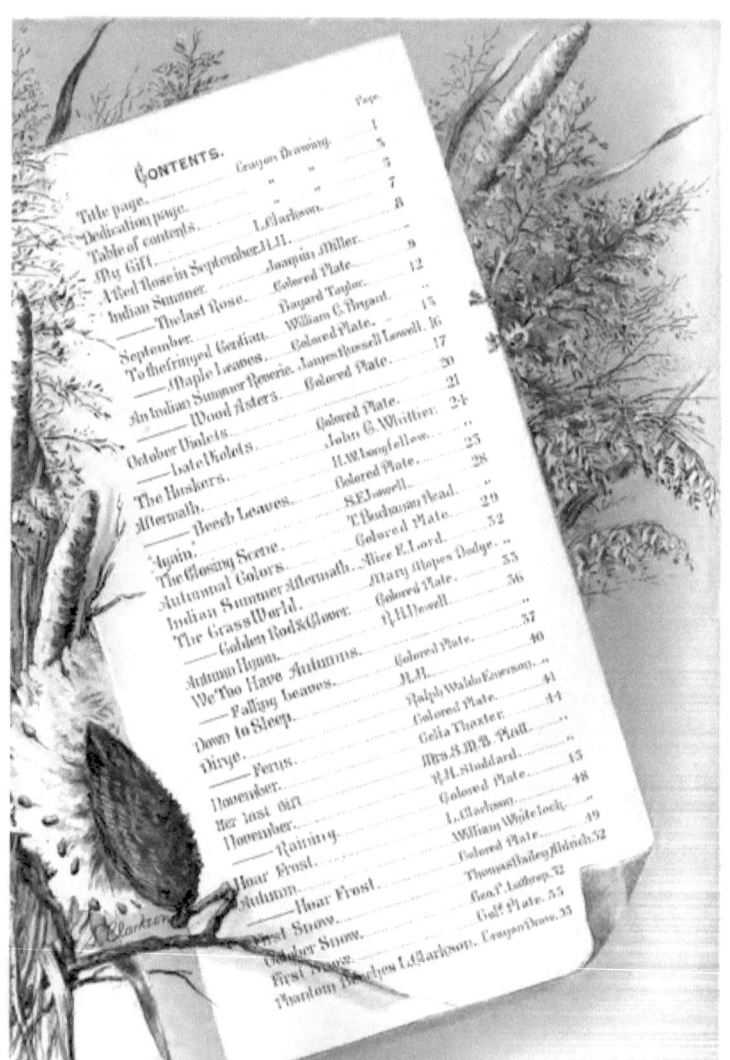

CONTENTS.

MY GIFT.

HAVE not brought thee, Friend, this time,
My passing thought or random rhyme;
I choose a theme that, like a call,
Shall echo in the hearts of all:
Then spread my page, and wait to see
What gracious gifts will come to me,
To make my offering meet for thee.
I ask my Woods to paint the strange
And subtle beauty of their change:
And, lo! beneath my hand I trace
The very look of Nature's face:—
This to my Book shall give its grace.
I ask the Poets for their songs,
And each one drops where it belongs
A feather from his ready wing—
For Poets soar the while they sing:
These to my Book its worth shall bring.

And last of all, before I send
My Gift, *that thou mayest love me, Friend,*
And not that thou wilt grant me fame,
I pause and write for thee my name
Upon a flower, across a leaf,
To speak my message bright and brief:
For thee may Indian Summer days
Be crowned with love and light and praise,
When hope and passion are but ember,
Sweeter than June be thy November;
Brighter, because the sunset land
That knows no shadow is at hand;
Richer, for harvesting is done,
And life's long effort has been won;
And gay desire and sodden grief
Have vanished with the scarlet leaf.
For with our Autumn comes this truth:
Contentment is not born of youth,
And Memory can more joy disclose
Than Hope in all her heyday knows.

7

A RED ROSE IN SEPTEMBER.

H. H.

O WILD red rose! What spell has stayed
  Till now thy summer of delights?
Where hid the south wind when he laid
  His heart on thine, these autumn nights?

O wild red rose! Two faces glow
  At sight of thee, and two hearts share
All thou and thy south wind can know
  Of sunshine in this autumn air.

O sweet wild rose! O strong south wind!
  The sunny roadside asks no reasons
Why we such secret summer find,
  Forgetting calendars and seasons!

Alas, red rose! Thy petals wilt;
  Our loving hands tend thee in vain;
Our thoughtless touch seems like a guilt;
  Ah, could we make thee live again!

Yet joy, wild rose! Be glad, south wind!
  Immortal wind! Immortal rose!
Ye shall live on in two hearts shrined,
  With secrets which no words disclose!

IN THE INDIAN SUMMER.

JOAQUIN MILLER.

THE squirrels chattered in the leaves,
The turkeys call'd from paw-paw wood,
The deer with lifted nostrils stood,
And humming-birds did wind and weave,
Swim round about, dart in and out,
Through fragrant forest edge made red,
Made many colored overhead
By climbing blossoms sweet with bee
And yellow rose of Cherokee.
Then frost came by and touched the leaves;
Then time hung ices on the eaves;
Then cushion-snows possessed the ground,
And so the seasons kept their round,
Yet still old Morgan went and came
From cabin door to forest dim,
Through wold of snows, through wood of flame,
Through golden Indian-Summer days
Hung round in soft September haze;—
And no man crossed or questioned him.

. . . .

8

The Last Rose

SEPTEMBER.

TO THE FRINGED GENTIAN.

SEPTEMBER.

BAYARD TAYLOR.

WHEN the maple turns to crimson,
  And the beechen leaves to gold;
When the gentian's in the meadow,
  And the aster on the wold;
When the noon is lapped in vapor,
  And the night is frosty cold;

Through the rustling woods I wander,
  Through the jewels of the year,
From the yellow uplands calling,
  Seeking her that is so dear:
She is near me in the Autumn,—
  She, the beautiful, is near.
      .   .   .   .

And I think when days are sweetest
  And the world is wholly fair,
She may sometimes steal upon me
  Through the dimness of the air,
With the cross upon her bosom
  And the amaranth in her hair.

TO THE FRINGED GENTIAN.

WILLIAM CULLEN BRYANT.

THOU blossom bright with autumn dew,
And covered with the heaven's own blue.
That openest when the quiet light
Succeeds the keen and frosty night.

Thou comest not when violets lean
O'er wandering brooks and springs unseen,
Or columbines, in purple dressed,
Nod o'er the ground-bird's hidden nest.

Thou waitest late, and com'st alone,
When woods are bare and birds are flown,
And frosts and shortening days portend
The aged year is near his end.

Then doth thy sweet and quiet eye
Look through its fringes to the sky,
Blue—blue—as if that sky let fall
A flower from its cerulean wall.

I would that thus, when I shall see
The hour of death draw near to me,
Hope blossoming within my heart,
May look to heaven as I depart.

L. Clarkson

Maple Leaves.

JAMES RUSSELL LOWELL.

WHAT visionary tints the year puts on,
When falling leaves falter through motionless air
Or numbly cling and shiver to be gone!
How shimmer the low flats and pastures bare,
As with her nectar Hebe Autumn fills
The bowl between me and those distant hills,
And smiles and shakes abroad her misty, tremulous hair!

No more the landscape holds its wealth apart,
Making me poorer in my poverty,
But mingles with my senses and my heart;
My own projected spirit seems to me
In her own reverie the world to steep;
'Tis she that waves to sympathetic sleep,
Moving as she is moved, each field and hill and tree.

How fuse and mix, with what unfelt degrees,
Clasped by the faint horizon's languid arms,
Each into each the hazy distances!
The softened season all the landscape charms;
Those hills, my native village that embay,
In waves of dreamier purple roll away,
And floating in mirage seem all the glimmering farms.

Far distant sounds the hidden chickadee
Close at my side; far distant sound the leaves;
The fields seem fields of dreams, where Memory
Wanders like gleaning Ruth; and as the sheaves
Of wheat and barley wavered in the eye
Of Boaz as the maiden's glow went by,
So tremble and seem remote all things the sense receives.
            .   .   .   .

O'er yon bare knoll the pointed cedar shadows
Drowse on the crisp, gray moss; the ploughman's call
Creeps faint as smoke from black, fresh-furrowed meadows;
The single crow a single caw lets fall;
And all around me every bush and tree
Says Autumn's here, and Winter soon will be,
Who snows his soft, white sleep and silence over all.

The birch, most shy and lady-like of trees,
Her poverty, as best she may, retrieves,
And hints at her foregone gentilities
With some saved relics of her wealth of leaves;
The swamp-oak, with his royal purple on,
Glares red as blood across the sinking sun,
As one who proudlier to a falling fortune cleaves.

16

Wood Asters

OCTOBER VIOLETS.

OCTOBER VIOLETS.

WE stood at the edge of the forest.
  The friend of my heart and I,
Where the sunset glow of the dogwood
  Met the sunset glow of the sky.

The breath of the coming winter
  Came down from the pine-clad hill ;
Its shadow crept over the landscape
  And over our hearts its chill.

We talked of our sunny childhood.
  Of hopes that long ago
We had watched with the opening blossoms
  As lightly come and go.

The dreams of our early morning
  Like the dew had passed away;
Our skies of gold and crimson
  Had turned to cloud and gray.

In the years that lay before us,
  Half seen through the distant haze,
The winters grew drearily longer,
  And briefer the summer days.

Like a breath from the far-off Southland
  Came a fragrance faint and sweet,
And behold !—blue violets nestled
  Low down in the grass at our feet.

As brightly they bloomed in their beauty
  At the close of this autumn day,
As when they were tenderly nestled
  In the cherishing arms of May.

Then one to the other spoke softly.
  "Oh, friend ! let our grievings cease :
Let us take to our hearts this message
  Of summer time and peace ;

" Let us lift our eyes to the future
  With a steady, trustful gaze ;
For violets still are waiting
  To bloom in October days."

October Violets

THE HUSKERS.

AFTERMATH.

JOHN G. WHITTIER.

It was late in mild October, and the long autumnal rain
Had left the summer harvest-fields all green with grass again.
The first sharp frosts had fallen, leaving all the woodlands gay
With the hues of summer's rainbow on the meadow-flowers of May.

Through a thin dry mist, that morning, the Sun rose broad and red,
At first a rayless disk of fire, he brightened as he sped ;
Yet even his noontide glory fell chastened and subdued
On the cornfields and the orchards and softly pictured wood.

And all the quiet afternoon, slow sloping to the night,
He wove with golden shuttle the haze with golden light ;
Slanting through the painted beeches he glorified the hill,
And beneath it pond and meadow lay brighter, greener still.

And shouting boys in woodland haunts caught glimpses of that sky,
Flecked by the many-tinted leaves, and laughed, they knew not why.
And school-girls, gay with aster-flowers, beside the meadow brooks
Mingled the glow of autumn with the sunshine of sweet looks.

From spire and barn looked westerly the patient weather-cocks ;
But even the birches on the hill stood motionless as rocks.
No sound was in the woodlands save the squirrel's dropping shell,
And the yellow leaves among the boughs, low rustling as they fell.

AFTERMATH.

HENRY W. LONGFELLOW.

When the summer fields are mown,
When the birds are fledged and flown,
    And the dry leaves strew the path ;
With the falling of the snow,
With the cawing of the crow
Once again the fields we mow,
    And gather in the aftermath.

Not the sweet, new grass with flowers
Is this harvesting of ours ;
    Not the upland clover bloom ;
But the rowen mixed with weeds,
Tangled tufts from marsh and meads,
Where the poppy drops its seeds
    In the silence and the gloom.

24

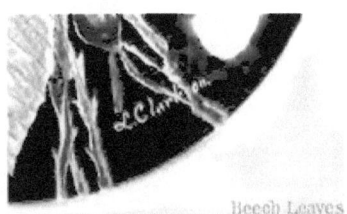

Beech Leaves

AGAIN.

THE CLOSING SCENE.

AGAIN.

N. E. LOWELL.

So soon, so soon, the summer leaves are turning
  To red and crimson, gold and russet brown ;
So soon again the maple's fires are burning,
  Lighting the hill-tops like a burnished crown—
  Far off within the shadowy mist
  Gleam purple, gold, and amethyst.

So soon, so soon, the summer leaves are dying,
  The fair, green leaves that lived their little day
In joyous freedom, now around us lying,
  Fading like many an earthly joy away—
  And flutt'ring through the charmèd air,
  Trail golden splendors everywhere.

All gorgeous hues, all dyes of Tyrian splendor
  Blossom and burn beneath the Master's hand ;
They thrill us, fill us with a joy so tender
  We reverent walk, as in some sacred land ;
  Or stand with claspèd hands to gaze
  Upon the glory of these sad, sweet days.

O far-off hills ! methinks your misty glory
  Leads upward to the Eternal hills of Gold,
Where earth's decay, nor sin's unhallowed story,
  Can vex nor mar the souls that ne'er grow old.
  O Summer Land ! we long for thee,
  Bend down that we thy gates may see.

—— · ——

From "THE CLOSING SCENE."

T. BUCHANAN READ.

Within his sober realm of leafless trees
  The russet year inhaled the dreamy air ;
Like some tanned reaper in his hour of ease,
  When all the fields are lying brown and bare.

All sights were mellowed and all sounds subdued,
  The hills seemed farther and the streams sang low ;
As in a dream the distant woodman hewed
  His winter log with many a muffled blow.

The embattled forests, erewhile armed in gold,
  Their banners bright with every martial hue,
Now stood, like some sad beaten host of old,
  Withdrawn afar in Time's remotest blue.

Autumnal Colors.

INDIAN-SUMMER'S AFTERMATH.

THE GRASS-WORLD.

INDIAN-SUMMER'S AFTERMATH.

ALICE E. LORD.

O DREAMY days that linger
  With trace of summer yet!
So soft, so mild, so mellow,
  Though breathing a regret!
Ye come, like farewell kisses,
  When love must soon grow strange—
That cling with painful fervor
  And bode the bitter change.

Ye come, with added glory
  Of red and amber sheen—
The Summer's ripened beauty,
  To supplement her green.
Ye pour this glory on us
  In the sweet days of rest,
That our regret may deepen
  To find the last, the best.

O peaceful days and golden!
  Ye call back summer flowers,
For daisies and red clover
  Peep out to count your hours.
Midst golden-rod and asters,
  They wander, wondering
To see the autumn banners
  Beneath the skies of spring.

So, into hearts well ripened
  Spring joys may bloom again,
And tangled cares and losses
  Find hope amid their pain.
That clover is the sweetest
  Which blushes in the fall;
That happiness completest
  Which comes the last of all.

OCTOBER, 1879.

FROM "THE GRASS-WORLD."

MARY MAPES DODGE.

AH, the grass-world dies in the autumn days,
  When, studded with sheaf and stack,
The fields lie browning in sullen haze,
  And creak in the farmer's track.
Hushed is the tumult the daisies knew,—
  The hidden sport of the supple crew;
  And lonely and dazed, in the glare of day,
  The stiff-kneed hoppers refuse to play
In the stubble that mocks the blue.
  For all things feel that the time is drear
  When life runs low in the heart of the year.

32

AUTUMN HYMN.

WE, TOO, HAVE AUTUMNS.

AUTUMN HYMN.

RICHARD H. NEWELL.

CHANGING, fading, falling, flying,
From the homes that gave them birth,
Autumn leaves, in beauty dying,
Seek the mother-breast of Earth.

Soon shall all the songless wood
Shiver in the deepening snow,
Mourning in its solitude,
Like some Rachel in her woe.

Slowly sinks yon evening sun,
Softly wanes the cheerful light,
And, the twelve hours' labor done,
Onward comes the solemn night.

So, on many a home of gladness,
Falls, O Death, thy winter gloom ;
Stands there still in doubt and sadness
Many a Mary at the tomb.

But the genial Spring, returning,
Will the sylvan pomp renew ;
And the new-born flame of morning
Kindle rainbows in the dew.

So shall God, His promise keeping,
To the world by Jesus given,
Wake our loved ones, sweetly sleeping,
At the opening dawn of heaven.

Light from darkness ! Life from death !
Dies the body, not the soul.
From the chrysalis beneath
Soars the spirit to its goal.

.   .   .   .   .   .

— ••• —

AUTUMN.

WE, too, have our Autumns when our leaves
Drop loosely through the dampened air ;
When all our good seems bound in sheaves,
And we stand reaped and bare.

Our seasons have no fixed returns ;
Without our will they come and go ;
At noon our sudden Summer burns—
Ere sunset, all is snow.

But each day brings less Summer cheer,
Cramps more our ineffectual Springs,
And something earlier, every year,
Our singing birds take wings.

" DOWN TO SLEEP."

DIRGE.

"DOWN TO SLEEP."

H. H.

November woods are bare and still,
November days are clear and bright;
Each noon burns up the morning's chill;
The morning's snow is gone by night;
Each day my steps grow slow, grow light,
As through the woods I reverent creep,
Watching all things lie "down to sleep."

I never knew before what beds,
Fragrant to smell, and soft to touch,
The forest sifts and shapes and spreads;
I never knew before how much
Of human sound there is in such
Low tones as through the forest sweep
When all wild things lie "down to sleep."

Each day I find new coverlids
Tucked in, and more sweet eyes shut tight;
Sometimes the viewless mother bids
Her ferns kneel down, full in my sight;
I hear their chorus of "good night,"
And half I smile, and half I weep,
Listening while they lie "down to sleep."

November woods are bare and still;
November days are bright and good;
Life's noon burns up life's morning chill;
Life's night rests feet which long have stood;
Some warm, soft bed, in field or wood,
The mother will not fail to keep,
Where we can "lay us down to sleep."

DIRGE.

RALPH WALDO EMERSON.

Knows he who tills this lonely field,
  To reap its scanty corn,
What mystic fruit his acres yield
  At midnight and at morn?

In the long sunny afternoon,
  The plain was full of ghosts;
I wandered up, I wandered down,
  Beset by pensive hosts.

But they are gone,—the holy ones,
  Who trod with me this lovely vale;
The strong, star-bright companions
  Are silent, low, and pale.

NOVEMBER.

HER LAST GIFT.

NOVEMBER.

NOVEMBER.

CELIA THAXTER.

THERE is no wind at all to-night
 To dash the drops against the pane;
No sound abroad, nor any light;
 And softly falls the autumn rain.

The earth lies tacitly beneath,
 As it were dead to joy or pain;
It does not move, it does not breathe;
 And softly falls the autumn rain.

And all my heart is patient too.
 I wait till it shall wake again;
For songs of Spring shall sound anew
 Though sadly falls the autumn rain.

HER LAST GIFT.

MRS. S. M. B. PIATT.

COME here. I know while it was May
 My mouth was your most precious rose,
My eyes your violets, as you say.
 Fair words, as old as Love, are those.

I gave my Flowers while they were sweet,
 And sweetly you have kept them all,
Through my slow Summer's great last heat
 Into the lonely mist of Fall.

Once more I give them. Put them by,
 Back in your memory's faded years—
Yet look at them, sometimes; and try,
 Sometimes, to kiss them through your tears.

NOVEMBER.

R. H. STODDARD.

THE wild November comes at last
 Beneath a veil of pain;
The night-wind blows its folds aside,—
 Her face is full of pain.

The latest of her race, she takes
 The Autumn's vacant throne:
She has but one short moon to live,
 And she must live alone.

It is no wonder that she comes,
 Poor month! with tears of pain;
For what can one so hopeless do
 But weep, and weep again?

44

November Rain

HOAR FROST.

AUTUMN.

HOAR FROST.

L. CLARKSON.

A SUDDEN grief was in the air ;
  A sigh came out of the wood ;
A white hand beckoned across the trees,—
  They shivered, and understood.

Was it a bevy of woodland elves,
  All dressed in red and brown,
That hurried through the chestnut boughs
  And flung the dried burs down ?

Was it a flock of frightened birds,—
  Brown birds with crimson breasts,—
That scurried by in reckless flight,
  With snow upon their crests ?

Or were they shadows of autumn days
  That passed in thronging hosts ?
The pensive and the golden hours,—
  Sober or ruddy ghosts.

Perhaps the spirits of summer flowers
  Were flitting overhead,
The white-winged seeds of thistles, and
  The souls of roses red :

A helpless and bewildered crowd,
  They lured me to a race ;
Over the fields with a gust behind,
  We went in headlong chase.

And I caught a brown and startled thing
  That in my face was toss'd ;
I smiled—for 'twas only a chestnut leaf
  Dashed with a white hoar frost.

AUTUMN.

WILLIAM WHITELOCK.

OLD AGE with joy and sorrow fills the cup
  From which its children drink from day to day ;
Yet sorrow to the surface coming up
  We deem it bitter, and would turn away ;

Forgetting that it sanctifies the soul,
  Its wisdom clears and purifies the sight ;
So calmly we will view the earthly goal
  Which shuddering childhood turned from with affright.

The leaves of Autumn, ere they reach the ground,
  Assume a beauty differing from the Spring ;
So manhood's Autumn, when by Virtue crowned,
  Should to the soul a calm enjoyment bring.

Hoar Frost.

FIRST SNOW.

OCTOBER SNOW.

FIRST SNOW.

THOMAS BAILEY ALDRICH.

THE summer comes and the summer goes,
  Wild flowers are fringing the dusty lanes,
  The sparrows go darting through fragrant rains,
And, all of a sudden—it snows!

Dear Heart! our lives so happily flow,
  So lightly, we heed not the flying hours ;
  We only know winter is gone—by the flowers,
We only know winter is come—by the snow!

***

OCTOBER SNOW.

TO LONGFELLOW ON HIS SEVENTIETH BIRTHDAY.

GEORGE P. LATHROP.

CAME once a dim October night
  So still the season's quiet flow
Seemed there to pause, as if it might
  In ripples back to summer go.

The heavy dusk in dreams like flowers
  Unfolded thoughts of endless ease :
Loss was no more ; life's coming hours
  Drove winter hence with melodies.

But keen-eyed Day through frostier air
  Beheld a swift age overgrow
Those flower-like dreams—for everywhere
  The night had whitened into snow!

Yet youthful still the trees arose ;
  And leaves consumed with autumn-fire
Blushed underneath the scattered snows
  With colors of the spring's desire.

And still with sweet defiance rang
  A late-voiced songster's echoing note :
Time altered not the strain he sang,
  Nor quenched the summer in his throat.

So in the days of youth you wrought
  A spell with Voices of the Night,
And left our hearts with flower-dreams fraught,
  And hush'd the easons in their flight.

And if too soon the hoar frost throngs
  Your air, O Poet of our prime,
It seeks in vain to chill your songs
  Or blanch the beauty of your rhyme!

The First Snow